Modern Publishing
A Division of Unisystems, Inc.
New York, New York 10022
Printed in Italy

Fisher-Price®

Favorite Lullabies

Modern Publishing
A Division of Unisystems, Inc.
New York, New York 10022
Series UPC #: 39640

Rock-a-bye, Baby

Rock-a-bye, baby,
On the treetops.
When the wind blows,
The cradle will rock.

When the bough breaks,
The cradle will fall,
And down will come baby,
Cradle, and all.

Brahms' Lullaby

Lullaby and good night!
With roses bedight,
With lilies o'erspread
Is my baby's wee bed.
Lay thee down now and rest.
May thy slumber be blessed.
Lay thee down now and rest.
May thy slumber be blessed.

I See the Moon

I see the moon, and the moon sees me.
The moon sees the one that I want to see.

Twinkle, Twinkle

Twinkle, twinkle, little star.
How I wonder what you are!
Up above the world so high,
Like a diamond in the sky,
Twinkle, twinkle, little star.
How I wonder what you are!

Sleep, Baby, Sleep

Sleep, baby, sleep.
Thy father guards the sheep.
Thy mother shakes the dreamland tree,
And down fall happy dreams for thee.
Sleep, baby, sleep.

Sleep, baby, sleep.
The large stars are the sheep.
The little stars are the lambs, I guess,
And the bright moon
   is the shepherdess.
Sleep, baby, sleep.

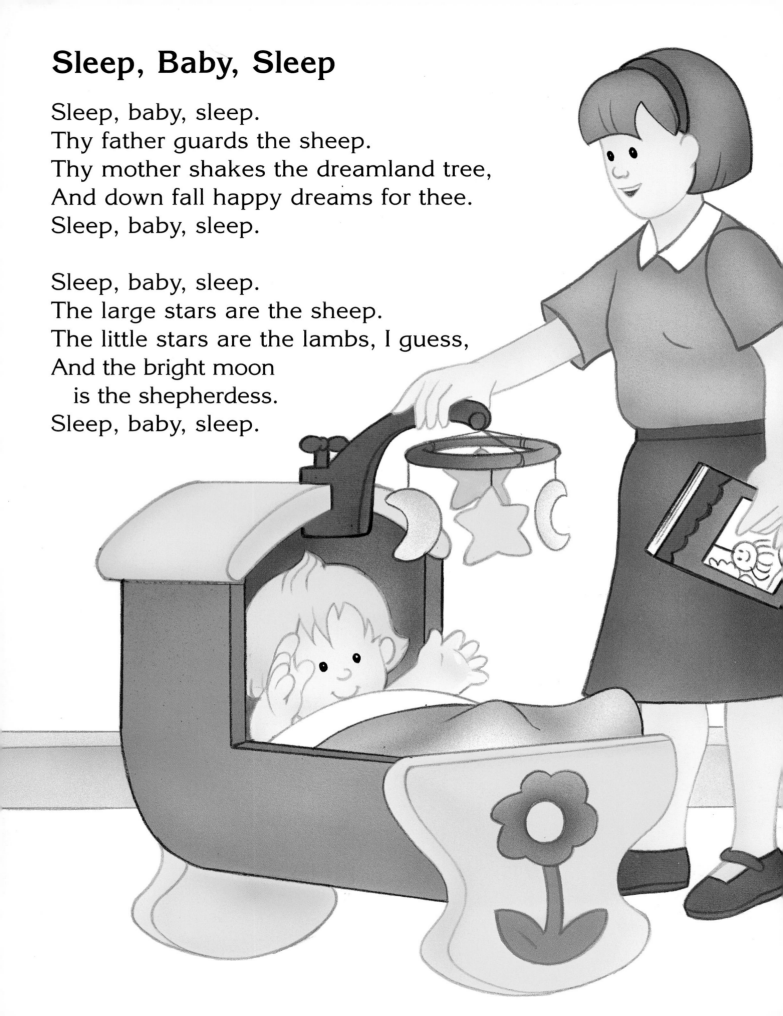

Mozart's Lullaby

Sleep, baby, sleep, and good night.
All the birds are asleep out of sight.
Quiet the lambs on the hill;
Even the bumble-bee's still.

Only the man in the moon
Still is a-nodding, but soon
Over him slumber will creep.
Sleep, baby, sleep, go to sleep.
Good night. Good night.

All the Pretty Horses

Hush-a-bye, don't you cry.
Go to sleep, my little baby.
When you wake, you shall have
All the pretty little horses:
Black and bay, dapple and gray,
Coach and six white horses.

Mammy loves, and pappy loves,
And Mammy loves her little baby.
Go to sleep, go to sleep,
Go to sleep, my little baby.
Black and bay, dapple and gray,
All the pretty little horses.

Hush, Little Baby

Hush, little baby, don't say a word.
Mama's gonna buy you a mockingbird.
And if that mockingbird don't sing,
Mama's gonna buy you a diamond ring.
If that diamond ring turns brass,
Mama's gonna buy you a looking-glass.
If that looking-glass gets broke,
Mama's gonna buy you a billy-goat.

If that billy-goat won't pull,
Mama's gonna buy you a cart and bull.
If that cart and bull turn over,
Mama's gonna buy you a dog named Rover.
If that dog named Rover won't bark,
Mama's gonna buy you a horse and cart.
If that horse and cart fall down,
You'll still be the sweetest little baby in town.

Bye, Baby Bunting

Bye, baby bunting,
Daddy's gone a-hunting
To get himself a rabbit skin
To wrap his baby bunting in.

Evening

The evening is coming, the sun sinks to rest.
The crow is a-flying straight home to his nest.
"Caw!" says the crow as he flies overhead.
It's time little people were going to bed.

The flowers are dozing, the daisies all sleep.
Primroses are buried in slumber so deep.
Closed for the night are the roses so red.
It's time little people were going to bed.